Mrs Dumpling and Captain Duff were neighbours. Mrs Dumpling had a goat called McEllicot who was the naughtiest animal in the valley. Captain Duff had an octopus called McGruer who turned beautiful colours. McGruer was the best-behaved octopus in all the world — but Mrs Dumpling didn't think so, for she was always accusing him of some terrible mischief or other.

Mrs Dumpling and Captain Duff spent most of their time squabbling, until McGruer lent a helping tentacle — or eight!

McGRUER
and the
GOAT

By the same author

Tiger's Milk
The Great Ballagundi Damper Bake
Rummage
Duck Boy

McGRUER and the GOAT

Christobel Mattingley

illustrations by

Carol McLean-Carr

ANGUS & ROBERTSON PUBLISHERS

Creative writing programme assisted by the Literature Board of the Australia Council, the Federal Government's arts funding and advisory body.

ANGUS & ROBERTSON PUBLISHERS

Unit 4, Eden Park, 31 Waterloo Road, North Ryde, NSW, Australia 2113, and 16 Golden Square, London W1R 4BN, United Kingdom

First published in Australia by Angus & Robertson Publishers in 1987
First published in the United Kingdom by Angus & Robertson (UK) in 1987

National Library of Australia Cataloguing-in-publication data.

Mattingley, Christobel, 1931-
McGruer and the goat.
ISBN 0 207 15052 4.
I. McLean-Carr, Carol, 1948- . II. Title.
A823'.3

Typeset in 14 pt Plantin by Midland Typesetters
Printed in Australia by Globe Press

To Elizabeth, Lesley and Lisa and
all the Cushlas and their families,
for whom nothing is impossible,
especially Cushla Y and hers.

McGRUER
and the
GOAT

When is an octopus more useful than a goat? That is a question on which Mrs Dumpling and Captain Duff could not agree. Mrs Dumpling and Captain Duff were neighbours. They lived in a valley high up in the hills way down south in Otago.

Mrs Dumpling kept black sheep which had the warmest wool in Otago and she had an apple tree which had the juiciest apples. She also had a goat called McEllicot. McEllicot gave the richest milk in Otago. But McEllicot was also the most mischievous goat in all the mountains, always meddling in other people's affairs.

Captain Duff kept bees which made the sweetest honey in Otago and he had a plum tree which grew the juiciest plums. He also had an octopus called McGruer. McGruer gave the biggest frights in Otago. But McGruer was also the best-behaved octopus in all the world, especially good at minding his own business.

Mrs Dumpling had lived in the valley all her life. And she knew all the stories of its babies, its brides, its grandfathers and its ghosts. Captain Duff had grown up in the valley and he had come back after a life at sea, with a head full of travellers' tales.

He longed to hear what had happened in the valley in all the years he had been away. And Mrs Dumpling longed to know about life beyond. But she did not like to tell the stories she knew, lest Captain Duff think she was a gossip. And he feared to tell of his travels, lest she think he was boasting.

And so they argued instead.

Mrs Dumpling said, "A goat has half as many legs and double the sense of an octopus."

Captain Duff said, "An octopus has twice as many legs and none of the nonsense of a goat."

And they were both much more lonely than they need have been.

The black sheep lived under the apple tree. The bees had a hive under the plum tree. McEllicot had a house of her very own by Mrs Dumpling's gate. But McGruer curled up in the chimney corner of Captain Duff's wee bach. And every time Mrs Dumpling came to visit he gave her a fright.

He didn't mean to. But she scared him first. It wasn't his fault if she always forgot he looked like a big brown cushion, and when she went to sit on him, naturally he would turn white with fright, white as a goat. After all, who wants to be sat on by someone as plump as Mrs Dumpling?

Then Mrs Dumpling and Captain Duff would begin to argue and McGruer would crawl into the chimney.

Go to page 12

"I do declare," Mrs Dumpling would say, "that octopus of yours will be the death of me yet. My heart is bleating like McEllicot."

Captain Duff would wink at McGruer, who would wink back from the chimney where he was turning sooty black.

Mrs Dumpling would puff, "And what on earth is the use of an outlandish creature like an octopus?"

Then Captain Duff would retort, "And what is the use of that goat of yours? I'll freeze to death if she keeps eating my long johns off the line. And I'll starve to death if she keeps upsetting my bees."

Mrs Dumpling would reply, "But her milk makes the best cheese and McGruer only curdles my blood."

"McGruer keeps me company," Captain Duff would say. And he couldn't think of a better answer.

But Mrs Dumpling would say, "McEllicot keeps me busy." And that was always the last word, because she would bustle back to her house to go on being busy. She loved being busy.

She spun the black sheep's wool and knitted caps and scarves and mittens which were famous among skiers and hikers. She baked the best apple pies and boiled the best apple dumplings in Otago. And she made the best cheese in all the Alps. Winter, summer, spring and autumn, she was always busy.

Captain Duff was different. He was used to watching the stars and waiting for the tides. He liked watching and waiting. He liked sitting and contemplating. In the spring he sat in the sun and watched the plum blossoms open. He watched the bees fly to and fro collecting nectar and transferring pollen. He watched the petals fall and in the summer he watched the plums grow, changing from green to purple.

In the autumn he waited for the wind which brought the fat plums falling and the sun which shrivelled the topmost to wrinkled prunes. And in the winter as he watched the snow creep down the mountainside, he waited for the plums to permeate the brandy in the big stone jar by the door, and as he waited he sipped some of last year's. It was the best plum brandy in all Otago.

Mrs Dumpling would bring Captain Duff presents – a balaclava she had knitted, an apple pie with crimpy edges and a pot of cream to eat with it, or a cheese as round and as pale as the full moon. And he would give her a jar of honey or a wee bottle of plum brandy, and a bag of prunes for McEllicot.

But she never brought anything for McGruer.

"I can't abide that octopus of yours," she would sniff. "And what good is he, anyway?"

"He's as good as a kaleidoscope, changing his colour a dozen times a day. It's never dull with him around," Captain Duff would say. "Camouflage, you know," he would explain.

"Kaleidoscopes, camouflage," Mrs Dumpling would sniff even louder. "What useless goings on! If you ask me, a goat is white, a black sheep is black, apples are red, and that's that."

Captain Duff would smile at McGruer and stroke him, and McGruer would turn pink with pleasure.

Mrs Dumpling would snort and hurry home to milk McEllicot.

But McEllicot was not often home. The black sheep browsed under the plum tree as well as the apple

tree – the grass seemed greener there – and kept it short so that it was easy to find the fallen fruit. The bees buzzed from tree to tree. After all, blossom was blossom to them and the fruit was all the better for it. But McEllicot roamed further afield, ranging the hillsides.

The mountains were a challenge to her and she loved to bleat her triumph from the crags. So the valley would often echo to the coaxing calls of Mrs Dumpling, ready with her stool and bucket, while McEllicot still frisked on a peak in the dawn or sunset.

Only McGruer stayed at home, brushing down cobwebs from the corners, watching the washing in case McEllicot took a fancy to it, guarding the beehive in case McEllicot decided to do a highland fling on it, acting as a scarecrow when the plums were ripening. Captain Duff would say, "I don't know what I'd do without you." Then McGruer would feel as treasured as a prospector's most prized specimen and become as speckled as a rock with gold.

One summer day as McGruer was lurking green as a leaf among the violets and irises along the path, quietly crunching snails, he noticed their silvery trails heading for Mrs Dumpling's strawberry patch and two of his tentacles reached after them.

Mrs Dumpling, on her way to the clothes line, saw them sliding through her plants. "Strawberry stealer!" she shouted and threw the peg bag at him.

McGruer was mortified at being misunderstood. He picked up two huge snails he had been about to eat and tossed them to Mrs Dumpling to show her what he was doing. They landed in her laundry basket right in the middle of her clean clothes.

HONEY

"You horrible creepy-crawly!" she shouted. "If you think that's funny, I don't. I'll teach you manners." And she seized the rake.

Captain Duff came hurrying to the commotion.

"I've caught that nasty beast of yours red-handed. Just look at him!" Mrs Dumpling pointed.

McGruer's tentacles recoiling from the strawberry patch were indeed red. In fact he had turned red all over. Red with rage and all puffed up.

But Mrs Dumpling did not understand about octopuses. "Just look at him," she repeated. "Bloated with my strawberries!"

"Snails more likely," Captain Duff said.

"Then why is he all red?" Mrs Dumpling demanded. "It's my belief he's allergic to strawberries. And it serves him right." She piled on the guilt like cream. "Take your trespassing tentacles away and don't let them ever stray this way again."

McGruer swarmed up the plum tree like a gigantic red balloon on legs and a flock of birds which had hoped for a feast took off in fright.

Captain Duff grinned at him. "Allergic!" he laughed. "To her precious strawberries! What does she know about coral gardens and abalone and fish that fly?" He smacked his lips.

McGruer grinned back and turned pale green dappled with gold, like water in a pool with the sun dancing on it, or leaves moving in the breeze. And he smiled at Captain Duff as they heard Mrs Dumpling's cries echoing from the hillsides as she tried to coax McEllicot home.

Autumn came early and took Mrs Dumpling by surprise. The wind came over the mountains with a whoosh that whisked her washing clean off the line. McGruer rescued her petticoat from Captain Duff's outhouse, three pairs of knickers from his gatepost and her feather quilt from the top of the plum tree.

He knocked on her door, put them down, then retreated round the corner quickly. Mrs Dumpling was surprised to find her washing neatly folded on her doorstep. She looked about suspiciously. McEllicot was chewing the boot Captain Duff had thrown when she climbed his woodheap and made it collapse. "Thank you, McEllicot," Mrs Dumpling said. "That was thoughtful of you." She bent down to pick up her laundry.

There was a large rude sound behind her. Mrs Dumpling had never heard an octopus say "Humph!" and she thought it was McEllicot. She wagged her finger at the goat. "Now that's not manners," she said.

Usually McEllicot could do no wrong in Mrs Dumpling's eyes, and she was so astonished at the unexpected and undeserved reproof that she dropped the boot. McGruer reached out a quick tentacle and retrieved it, rippling with laughter as he went to share the joke with Captain Duff.

That night the wind came back with all its brothers and sisters. They whirled and whistled and whooped and did a war dance up and down the valley.

Captain Duff and McGruer knew all about tempests and typhoons, hurricanes and waves as high as houses. They smiled at each other, snug in their wee bach.

But Mrs Dumpling had lived all her life in the valley and in the sudden silence when the winds went off to fetch their aunts and uncles, she said to

Good book eh!

McEllicot, "I don't like the sound of it. Remember the story of the big storm when Grandfather's roof was carried clean over Ben Buchan? They say it was because he was fooled by the lull and he stayed in bed instead of going out and putting more stones on the roof. Out with you now, and up on the roof. Quick, quick!"

Clutching her shawl around her shoulders, she shoved the unwilling goat out into the darkness, taking no notice of McEllicot's cries, "But the trolls will get me!" She seized a basket, piled it full of cheeses, grabbed the ladder, propped it against the wall and heaved the loaded basket up onto the roof. She scrambled up after it and was putting out the last cheese when the winds came back, with their first and second and third cousins as well.

They tossed down the ladder, threw away the basket and picked up the cheeses, pelting each other and pitching them into the valley. Then they swooped on Mrs Dumpling, clinging to the gable with her skirts billowing about her, and McEllicot astride the ridge pole.

"Your turn," they shrieked, and Captain Duff and McGruer, awakened by the noise of cheeses rolling down their roof, looked out of their window to see Mrs Dumpling sailing through the air.

"Quick, quick! Here's our chance to prove that eight hands are better than two," Captain Duff exclaimed.

But McGruer needed no urging. He was already out in the dark grappling with the unseen forces of the winds. Up onto Mrs Dumpling's roof he writhed, twisting and turning his tentacles to deflect the winds'

snatching attacks. He stretched himself to his full extent, two arms to each side of the four-square roof, and all the blows and buffets in the world could not prise him loose or shift a single shingle. He clung with all the strength of every sucker, defying the winds which swore and spat at him with stinging rain, until at last they began to mutter defeat and slink away.

Meanwhile, Captain Duff, lantern in hand, had gone in search of Mrs Dumpling. He found her wedged in McEllicot's house in the hollow by the gate. But of McEllicot there was no sign.

They stumbled up the slope, stubbing their toes on cheeses, the basket and the ladder, back to Captain Duff's bach, where they sat drinking plum brandy and swapping storm stories until the sun rose through tattered clouds.

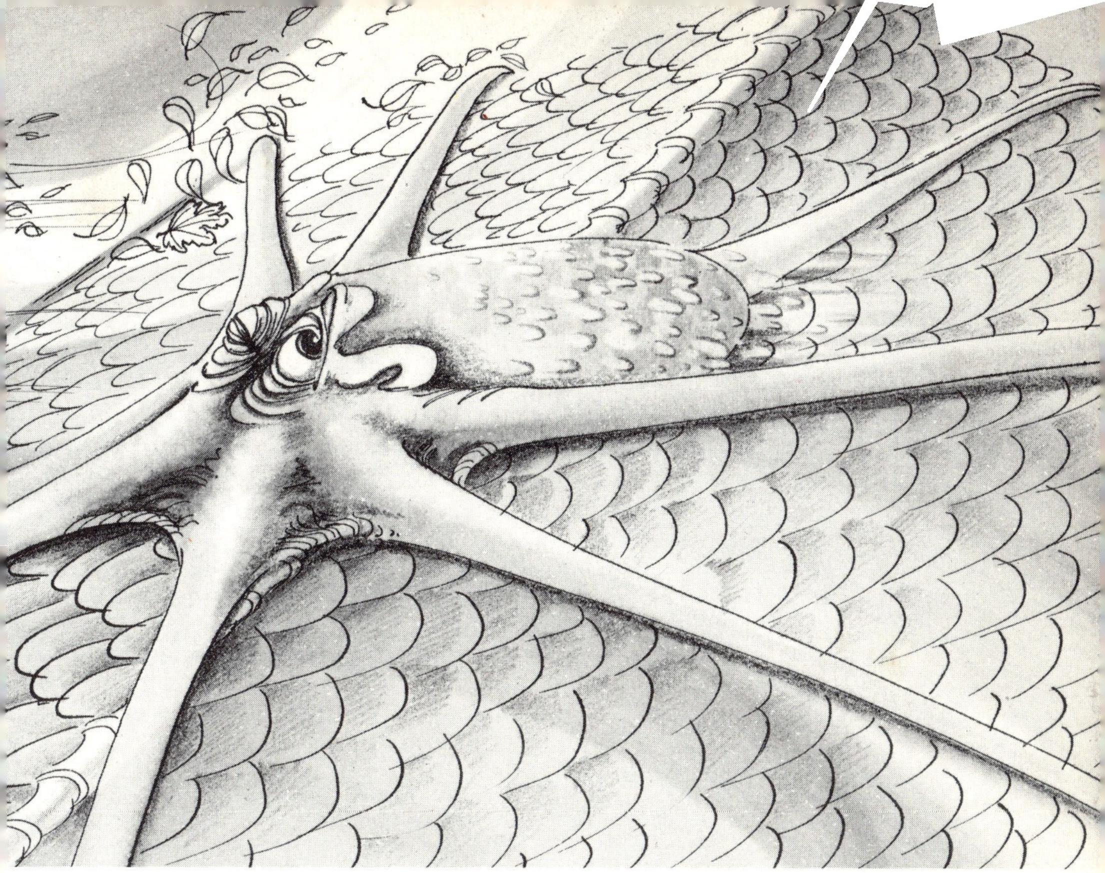

When they went outside to assess the damage on the valley's storm scale, Mrs Dumpling stared in amazement at McGruer, still crouched on her roof, from which not a shingle, not even a speck of moss was missing.

"Now that's a story to beat them all," she said and she shook with laughter like a dumpling bobbing in a pot of boiling water. Then quickly, in case the octopus might think she was laughing at him and become hurt or offended, she added, "Thank you kindly, Mr McGruer. It was good of you to lend a hand, or rather eight, to be precise. Please come down and let me shake them."

"He'd sooner be tickled," Captain Duff told her. So she tickled him shyly. And when he turned pink she did too.

"Now I must get busy," she said. "Come back at midday and have dinner with me."

McGruer was a tidy octopus, so he spent the morning rounding up the cheeses and stacking them neatly in the basket, while Captain Duff washed the plum brandy glasses and chuckled over the stories Mrs Dumpling had told.

As for Mrs Dumpling, she sang every song she knew while she made the biggest apple dumpling in all Otago and put it to cook in her largest pot. She stoked the fire so well, the water boiled so hard and the dumpling swelled so large that just before midday it swelled right out of the pot and up into the chimney.

When Captain Duff and McGruer arrived for dinner, smoke was pouring out of the door of Mrs Dumpling's house and tears were rolling down her cheeks.

"There's always tomorrow," Captain Duff said, "and McGruer will clear out your chimney in no time when it cools."

"But Mr McGruer is my guest of honour at dinner today. And now I can only give him bread and cheese." She wiped away her tears. "Never mind, there's nothing better than goat's milk cheese."

"Not goat's milk cheese," Captain Duff said. "Any other kind. But not goat's milk. McGruer is allergic to goat's milk cheese." He winked at McGruer.

"No one is allergic to goat's milk," Mrs Dumpling declared. "And this is the finest goat's milk cheese in Otago."

"Octopuses are supersensitive," Captain Duff said. "Besides, he doesn't like it. McGruer is used to dugong cheese and McEllicot is an acquired taste."

“Dugong cheese?” Mrs Dumpling was flustered. “I’m afraid I haven’t got any of that. I know then. Strawberry jam. I know he likes strawberries.”

“I know he doesn’t. Snails he likes, not strawberries. Strawberries make him sick.”

The thought of an octopus being sick in her kitchen was almost too much for Mrs Dumpling. But the thought of serving snails on one of her best blue and white china plates was also hard to swallow.

“I know you were telling me how people eat snails in France. But I thought you said he came from the South Seas. So what does he eat when he’s at home? I mean at home there, not at home here,” she enquired, anxious for her reputation as a hostess.

“Crabs for preference,” Captain Duff said.

“Now you’re talking,” Mrs Dumpling said. “I have the very thing. Crabs pickled after my grandmother’s recipe.” She put down a big crock in front of McGruer.

McGruer lifted the lid and pulled out a pickled crab-apple. He gurgled as he swallowed it and rolled his eyes at Captain Duff. But it was kindly meant, for after all what did she know of tropical islands and crabs which scuttled sideways under rocks instead of hanging by stalks on trees?

They settled down to celebrate the saving of the roof and the kitchen was soon filled with the sayings and doings of folk of the olden days, the air bright with images of faraway places. Captain Duff was just putting away the last slice of bread and cheese. McGruer had already licked out the last drops of Grandmother Dumpling’s secret syrup and was looking around. There were shelves stacked with cheeses, jars of apple jelly and enough knitted socks and gloves to have fitted him out eight times over.

Mrs Dumpling, who had already picked up her knitting, saw his wondering gaze and sighed. "McEllicot and I used to go to market once a week. I'd fill my cart with socks and cheeses and apple pies and McEllicot pulled it for me. I did such a good trade." She sighed again. "But McEllicot started to get a wee bit bored with being in the town. She ate the town clerk's roses, chased the schoolmaster up the street, climbed on the church roof and rang the bell. She loved the library and specially liked the encyclopaedias. She rode on the fire engine and hitchhiked on top of a bus. But it was the day she danced on the bar in the hotel that did it. She just refused to pull the cart after that.

"And even though the cart was light—I always used to sell everything . . . people would queue up for my apple pies," Mrs Dumpling said proudly, "—it's a long haul home up the hills. So I had to stop going to market.

"But I couldn't stop shearing my sheep and spinning and knitting their wool, could I? And the apples had to be picked, didn't they? I couldn't waste them, could I? So I made Aunt Mabel's apple jelly. It never fails to set. And it looks so pretty, doesn't it?" She smiled up at the rows and rows of ruby jars glowing on the shelf.

"As for the cheese, McEllicot is such a heavy milker. She just thrives on adventures. But it's time she was home now." Mrs Dumpling started to look anxious. "I hope the trolls haven't got her. She's such a ninny nanny of a goat."

"Not a chance," Captain Duff said stoutly. "I never

met a goat with more sense in all my travels. Did you, McGruer?"

McGruer waved a tentacle in agreement.

"And a goat with such good taste. I mean, where would she find anything more to her liking than on my clothes line?"

Mrs Dumpling laughed her rich, rumbling laugh. "You're right. McEllicot is not stupid. She's more than a match for all the trolls of Otago."

"It's my guess she'll be home to help polish off that apple dumpling as soon as McGruer gets it out of the chimney tomorrow," Captain Duff said with great certainty.

But she was not.

McGruer did a splendid job of cleaning out the chimney. And there was more than enough apple dumpling for two serves each. McGruer put aside a fair share for McEllicot, but only the bees came to taste it.

Mrs Dumpling was full of praise for McGruer's efforts. "I don't believe my chimney has been more thoroughly cleaned since your father did it," she said to Captain Duff. "There never was a better chimney sweep. We've certainly missed him in the district since he died. If Mr McGruer would like to carry on the family business, I'm sure folk would be very pleased. There must be a lot of chimneys overdue for a good sweep."

Captain Duff thought of all the stories he would hear sitting in kitchens waiting for McGruer. He was a glutton for stories. "What do you think?" he asked the octopus.

McGruer winked and went black.

"A wink is as good as a nod," Captain Duff said. "Let's go and look in the ceiling where my dad always kept his brushes."

Sure enough, the brushes were there. McGruer passed them down to Captain Duff who demonstrated. "Like this, McGruer." McGruer tried them out in Captain Duff's chimney.

They went across to tell Mrs Dumpling. There was a smell of apple pies coming from her kitchen.

"Won't you stay to lunch? I'm worried about McEllicot," she said all in one breath.

So they stayed and Captain Duff told some of his tales to keep her mind off what might have happened to McEllicot.

McGruer was full of apple dumpling, so he could manage only one apple pie, even though it was the most delicious he had ever tasted, with pastry that melted in the mouth and apples drooling with cinnamon and sugar. Captain Duff was so busy telling tales because he was hungry for a listener that he ate only one also, even though it was better than those his mother used to make. Mrs Dumpling was so busy listening because she was starved for stories of the wide wide world that she ate only one also, even though they were the best batch she had ever made, thanks to McGruer cleaning the chimney so well.

So there were thirty-three apple pies left on the table.

"What shall I do with them if McEllicot doesn't come home?" Mrs Dumpling wailed.

Captain Duff filled her tea cup and said, "Well now, if you were in Bombay I would say go to the bazaar . . ." and Mrs Dumpling forgot to worry as she began to listen again.

McGruer stole away from the table. He went to Mrs Dumpling's shed and found the cart McEllicot had refused to pull. He dragged it out into the autumn sunshine and brushed the dust off, then quietly took it down to her door.

Captain Duff was telling about Shanghai now and Mrs Dumpling had forgotten her tea cup, she had dropped her knitting and her eyes were bulging like crab-apple dumplings.

"You don't say, Captain Duff. Go on . . ."

Stealthily, silently, McGruer slipped in and lifted down piles of socks, packed them into the bottom of the cart, gently put a layer of apple pies on top, lovingly covered them with a layer of gloves, until with layer after layer the cart was almost full and the table was empty.

He had just lifted down two dozen jars of apple jelly to pack into the corners when the flash of ruby caught Mrs Dumpling's eye. She shrieked.

"Oh, Mr McGruer! What a fright you gave me. Careful of my jars. They'll break on this stone floor."

Captain Duff chuckled. "McGruer's not McEllicot. He won't drop them."

McGruer stretched out two tentacles proudly and displayed a dozen jars of apple jelly firmly fixed to each. "He's like those waiters in Marseilles I was telling you about," Captain Duff said, "the ones who can carry a dozen plates up their arms at a time."

"Well, I never!" was all Mrs Dumpling could say.

She watched McGruer pack the precious jars, then hitch himself into the shafts. "You've certainly got yourself a smart octopus, and no mistake."

"He's got me, more like it," Captain Duff said, patting McGruer who gave him a friendly squeeze.

"When I think of the trouble I used to have trying to harness up McEllicot! It was a proper circus!"

"Talking of circuses," Captain Duff said, "have you ever seen a Russian bear? Now when I was in Vladivostok . . ."

McGruer winked at Mrs Dumpling. She put fresh tea in the pot. McGruer sidled into a corner and began fiddling with the spinning wheel. Captain Duff went on talking. Mrs Dumpling took up her knitting again. And McGruer began to spin.

"Just look at that," Mrs Dumpling marvelled.

Captain Duff said, "He's like me. He likes a good yarn." And he and Mrs Dumpling laughed so loudly that the sound of it went over the hills and far away.

McEllicot heard it and wondered what fun she was missing. She started to head for home.

But she still hadn't arrived by next morning.

Mrs Dumpling hung the bucket and milking stool on hooks at the back of the cart. "You never know," she said.

"You're right," Captain Duff said cheerfully, shouldering the chimney brushes while McGruer hitched himself into the cart again. "That's the best part of setting sail. Anything could happen. Anchors aweigh!" he called.

Mrs Dumpling was a little nervous of saying, "Hold hard, my hearty," to an octopus, so she said, "Just a moment, please, Mr McGruer", leaned over him and popped a cap she had knitted onto his head. "To keep the soot out of your eyes," she said.

McGruer turned bright pink. It was the first time anyone had ever given him a present. He took it off,

admired it, then tucked it under his web, which was even better than a pocket for keeping things safe.

"It isn't that he doesn't like it," Captain Duff explained. "But his head will get hot while he pulls the cart and he perspires easily."

Mrs Dumpling looked astonished. "I never thought of an octopus perspiring! With all those arms too!"

"It's all right. You're upwind of him," Captain Duff assured her. And they all laughed so loudly that McEllicot heard it across two mountain ranges and began to hurry.

"Heave ho, my hearty," Captain Duff said. And they set off.

They caused quite a stir when they arrived in the market place. The locals flocked to buy Mrs Dumpling's apple pies, and they recognised Captain Duff with greetings which warmed his heart. But everyone kept their distance from McGruer.

He was just curling himself into a ball down the muzzle of the war memorial cannon where he hoped small boys with sticks wouldn't be able to reach him, when Mrs Dumpling came to his rescue.

She fancied herself now as something of an authority on octopuses and she explained at large what a good job McGruer had done on her chimney and how he was going into the family business as first assistant to Captain Duff. She called him to come out of the canon and as he emerged shyly from the long black barrel in front of the crowd, he was his own best advertisement. Together with Captain Duff, he received more offers of jobs than there are weeks in the year.

It was a very pleasurable and profitable day for all.

For the first time in his life McGruer was welcome in everyone's house and he felt thoroughly at home in the depths of the chimneys he visited. Captain Duff was at home too among people who had known him as a boy and he began to catch up on all that had happened in the valley while he had been sailing the seven seas.

Mrs Dumpling was in her element among all the people in the market and her socks and gloves were as popular as ever. Tourists from across the world talked to her and promised to send postcards of castles on the Rhine, tulips in Holland, temples in Japan and skyscrapers in New York.

She told Captain Duff about it on the way home. "I even sold three pairs of socks to a mountaineer from Chile."

"Then he's not silly," Captain Duff said. "No chilly blains for him."

Their laughter rang across the closest mountain and McEllicot on the other side put on an extra spurt.

When they got home Mrs Dumpling said to McGruer, "All that soot and sweat. Why don't you take a bath? I'll light just a wee fire under the copper to take the chill off the water for you."

McGruer had soaked every tentacle and scrubbed every sucker and was just wallowing lazily in the warm water, curling and uncoiling, when there was a loud clatter outside.

The door burst open and who should come in but McEllicot. She was just about to gobble down a bucketful of apples when McGruer squirted her with water. She skipped with surprise, looked around the

seemingly empty laundry and returned to the apples. McGruer squirted harder the second time and knocked an apple from her mouth. She bleated with annoyance and bent down to pick it up. McGruer squirted so hard the third time that McEllicot was drenched. Then he submerged in the sooty water in the copper, which bubbled like a mud pool with his laughter.

"Geysers and billy ghosts!" said McEllicot. "I'm getting out."

McGruer emerged from the copper and threw long shiny arms across the door. "No you're not," he said in a cavernous voice.

McEllicot jumped so high that she hit the roof. Coming down again, she recognised McGruer and began to bleat. "Oh, it's only you! What a fright you gave me." She stamped her foot and tossed her head.

McGruer laughed. "I'm glad. You deserved it." Then he became thoughtful. "But it's the first time I ever have been glad. I don't mean to frighten people and I don't like it when I do. I'm a shy sort of fellow really and I'd much sooner make friends. Where have you been?" he asked. "Mrs Dumpling has been worried."

"I went with the winds," McEllicot said.

"Where did they take you?" McGruer asked.

"Over the mountains and far far away."

"What did you see?"

"I saw the sea," McEllicot said. "Blue and shining and stretching as far into the distance as the mountains reach to the sky."

The octopus looked sad. "It's deep too," he said. "As deep as the mountains are high. And all sorts of creatures live in it and plants grow in it."

The goat looked at the octopus. "You'd like to see it again, wouldn't you?"

McGruer nodded.

"Then I'll take you," McEllicot announced. "It's a fair way to walk, and I wouldn't want to do it by myself again, because of the trolls. But I'd like to hear them say, 'Who's that walking over my bridge?' And I'd love to see their faces when you appear." She giggled. "Oh, I don't mean because you're ugly," she hastened to add. "Nobody can help their looks." She pirouetted, studying her dainty feet smugly.

Then she noticed that McGruer was going a dirty khaki.

"I mean that you're more than a match for any troll. You're so smart."

McGruer went pink. "Intelligence is a characteristic of the species," he said modestly.

He flexed his tentacles. "There's no doubt I could turn the tables on any troll. I could make my own bridge." He swung two pairs of tentacles from one side of the room to the other and with scarcely a contortion, minced the other four across the instant bridge. "Trip, trap, trip, trap," he warbled.

McEllicot couldn't stop giggling. "Oh, McGruer, you are so funny. The trolls would die laughing."

"A nice way to go," McGruer commented solemnly. And added, "A playful disposition has frequently been observed in octopuses in captivity." He shook himself back to his normal arrangement. "Not that I'm in captivity," he said quickly. "It's just that I'm the only company Captain Duff's got. He'd miss me terribly if I went off tramping. Besides, we've just taken up the family business again and there are enough chimneys to keep us busy every Friday for a year while Mrs Dumpling . . ."

"Friday?" McEllicot interrupted. "That's market day. You mean . . . Oh no!" She stamped. "I'm just going to put my foot right down, and not in front of that horrible, humiliating cart either. And I'm never going to set them in that boring market square again either. Why, what would I do? There's hardly a challenge left in the whole town. I could climb the cannon, but even the kids do that. I could eat the rope and bring the flag down. Not fully down – half-mast would make it more interesting. I could . . ."

McGruer said, "No need to be worried about that horrible, humiliating cart, as you call it. Of course it does squeak a bit, I grant you, which draws unnecessary attention. But a well-placed drop of oil will soon fix that. I might have a look at replacing the axle too. That would make it run more smoothly."

McEllicot's eyes widened. "You're quite an engineer, aren't you?"

"The octopus has also been observed to be both inquisitive and ingenious," McGruer remarked. "As for something to do, there's a lot of truth in the old proverb, 'Many hands make light work.' Mind you, I'm not saying Captain Duff doesn't play his part. He does. He chats up the clients. In fact you might say he's the chatting partner. But I do the real work and even I can't be in more than eight places at once. Now if we were to take you into the partnership as the rooftop inspector, some of my problems would be immediately eliminated. I shall put it to Captain Duff as my recommendation."

"You mean I'd be officially allowed on people's roofs?"

"Only on the roofs of clients. With their approval, of course. But I'm sure we'd have no problem there." He curled and uncurled his tentacles reflectively.

"McGruer!" McEllicot exclaimed. "If I could hug you, I would."

"McEllicot," McGruer replied, "allow me to return the compliment." And he did.

McEllicot looked at him with shining eyes. "That wasn't half as bad as I used to think it would be. In fact it was twice as good." Then she sighed. "But I still have a problem. If we're going off to the mountains for a couple of days . . ."

"Tell me," said McGruer. "The octopus is known to be innovative and adaptable. Problems are my meat and drink."

"Well, this one will have to be your drink," McEllicot said. "It's my milk. What'll we do with it, otherwise? And I really should be milked twice a day for comfort."

McGruer turned a sickly white. He could face the thought of a troll on its own ground. But goat's milk . . . twice a day . . . He tried not to heave and wondered if he really needed to see the sea so badly after all.

He heard McEllicot sniffle and turned to her. She was looking very uncomfortable indeed. "And I haven't been milked for two days now," she bleated miserably.

McGruer took pity on her. He picked up the bucket, emptied out the apples, coiled himself around her and said, "I'll try my hand at it."

McEllicot snuggled up against him and said,

"You're much more comfortable than a stool." The milk came down in warm sweet squirts and the bucket began to fill. Higher and higher the milk crept until the foam was tickling McGruer's mouth. He licked his lips without thinking. They tasted warm and sweet. The bucket was almost overflowing.

"Quick, what shall I do?" McGruer said. He looked around. There was not another container in sight.

"The octopus is known to be innovative and adaptable," McEllicot repeated dreamily. "So have a swig," she said, kicking his left hind tentacle sharply with her right forefoot.

McGruer swigged obediently. He swigged again. And again. "That wasn't half as bad as I used to think it would be. In fact it was twice as good." He licked his lips appreciatively. "Let's go up the mountains tomorrow." He turned pink in anticipation.

"We'd better go and tell Mrs Dumpling I'm home and Captain Duff we're going," McEllicot said primly, as if butter wouldn't melt in her mouth. "Though it doesn't sound as if she's worried about me now, and it certainly doesn't sound as if he'll miss you tomorrow," she observed, as the sounds of laughter and talk which had been coming from the kitchen continued unabated.

As they opened the door Mrs Dumpling was just reaching out for the teapot on the hob. "I don't know that I really want to go to Russia," she was saying, "but I wouldn't mind one of those samovars you were telling me about. Imagine, tea on tap all day long!" She picked up her empty cup.

McGruer put the bucket of milk down beside her.

PAINT

"I wouldn't be wishing for a samovar full of tea that rots your guts," he said, "when you've got a goat like McEllicot with the best milk in Otago on tap fresh twice a day."

Mrs Dumpling looked up. "McEllicot!" she shrieked. "What a fright you've given me! Mr McGruer, where did you find her? Thank you for bringing her home. And you've milked her too! How lovely!"

"My pleasure, Ma'am," McGruer said, and his voice was as smooth as plum brandy. "Contrary to its unfortunate reputation in the popular press, the octopus is friendly and cooperative, as well as diligent."

"And you talk as well!" Mrs Dumpling's mouth was so wide open, McGruer was tempted to stuff her ball of knitting wool into it to see what would happen next. He restrained himself however, and said firmly, more to himself than others, "Some octopuses have been described as pranksters. But one prankster in a family is enough." He smiled indulgently at McEllicot.

"You never told me that he could talk," Mrs Dumpling said to Captain Duff. "And where did he learn to milk, I'd like to know."

"Well, my dear Eva, I wish I could take you to that tropical paradise, that little island in the South Seas where the lagoons are as blue as mermaids' eyes, the palms sigh like lovesick sailors and the coconut milk is like the elixir of life."

"Thank you, Herbert, but I'm not much of a one for gadding about. And besides, who'd look after the sheep while I was away? You just tell me about it and I'll be happy."

And so it came to pass that as McEllicot and

McGruer tramped off up the mountainside for a view of the sea, Captain Duff sat in the sun with his telescope to his right eye and his back against the wall of his wee bach, telling the story of his first encounter with the octopus to Mrs Dumpling. And as she spun her wool and he spun his tale, he would break off from time to time as he caught a glimpse of them among the crags, and slap his knees with a shout of laughter that made the mountains ring.

"My McGruer and his skipping samovar! Every troll in Otago will be off to Norway tomorrow!" Then as they finally disappeared over the highest peak he added, "And I can't think of anything more useful than that. Unless it is an apple pie with a piece of goat's milk cheese."

THE GREAT BALLAGUNDI DAMPER BAKE

The little town of Ballagundi has a problem — a wheat glut. The silos are full to overflowing, and the people's pockets are empty! The situation seems hopeless — and then the Shire President has his Great Idea . . . an idea to save the day, an idea to bring the tourists and their dollars flocking — The Great Ballagundi Damper Bake!

Christobel Mattingley's marvellous tall tale has lively illustrations, rich in humorous detail, by Will Mahony. Available in the BLUEGUM paperback series for children.

RUMMAGE

Christobel Mattingley

Delightful dusty rummage cluttered Mr Portwine's market stall — teapots without lids and lids without teapots, coats without buttons and buttons without coats, pictures without frames and frames without pictures, lamps without shades and shades without lamps, odd knives, odd forks, odd earrings.

Mr Portwine's customers were mad about his jumble. But the other stallholders were not.

"Spruce yourself up a bit," barked Major Martindale of the military souvenirs stall.

"It lowers the whole tone," snorted Miss Sarah Snodgrass of antique dolls.

And so Mr Portwine decided to smarten himself up — with disastrous results.

Superbly illustrated by Patricia Mullins, *Rummage* was awarded the first Junior Reader's Medal in the Australian Children's Book Council Awards for 1982.

Available in paperback.

DUCK

BOY

Christobel Mattingley

Adam is feeling rather left out. He is on holiday at Mrs Perry's farm with his brother and sister who are having a wonderful time. But he is too young to go riding with Kate or canoeing with Steve — at least, that's what *they* say.

Then Adam discovers Lucy and The General, the ducks who live under the old willow by the creek. They need help.

They are trying to protect a clutch of eggs from the goannas and rats that plague them every year. They are menaced by the foxes that prowl among the blackberries. Adam is determined that this year, at least, Lucy and The General will raise their family in peace and safety.

Christobel Mattingley's warm, sensitive story is complemented by Patricia Mullins's delicate drawings.